KU-756-956

£1·35

Contents

Illustrations by Edgar Hodges David Fryer

Copyright © MCMLXXVII by Wombles Limited/ Filmfair Limited.
Based on the BBC-TV series.
Original text and character material © Elisabeth Beresford.
Original film puppet designs by Ivor Wood © Filmfair Limited.
All rights reserved throughout the world.
Published in Great Britain by
World Distributors (Manchester) Limited,
A member of the Pentos Group,
P.O. Box 111, 12 Lever Street, Manchester M60 1TS
Printed in Great Britain by Jarrold & Sons Ltd., Norwich.
SBN 7235 0434 2

Bungo and the yellow fog

by
Elisabeth Beresford

A thick yellow fog was rolling over Wimbledon Common. It came down so suddenly and with so little warning that all the young Wombles who were out on tidying-up work had hardly any time in which to escape from it.

Orinoco, who always tries to work as close to the burrow as possible, was the first home. He was closely followed by Wellington, who had been tidying-up so hard that he'd already set off for home a few minutes ahead of the fog. Tomsk came in next, puffing and blowing, for he had run as fast as possible as soon as he saw the yellow fog rolling towards him.

"OOO-ER," rumbled Tomsk, "that was horrible. Fog smells and tastes really nasty. OOO-ER!"

"Chuck up, young Womble," said Tobermory, hitting him on the back. "I've got the burrow air-cleaning machine going, so we won't have to worry about the fog in here. But hold on a minute, there's only three of you back. Where's Bungo?"

Everybody looked at everybody else, and then shook their heads.

"Sorry," said Wellington, "but the last I saw of Bungo he was hurrying off towards Queen's Mere. I say, Tobermory, supposing the fog catches him

5

and he starts choking? He might get really frightened, you know. Perhaps we'd better send out a search party. I'll volunteer to go and look for him."

"And me," rumbled Tomsk, wiping his eyes, which were still smarting from the fog.

"And me too, I suppose," agreed Orinoco with a heavy sigh.

"Very good of you," said Great Uncle Bulgaria, coming into the Workshop. "Well done. But although Bungo is a silly young Womble in many ways, I think he'll have the good sense to use his head and not panic. He has, after all, been trained to look after himself in moments of danger."

"Y-y-yes. Perhaps," said Wellington doubtfully, "but it is awfully nasty out on the Common, Great Uncle Bulgaria. S-sorry, but you don't know what it's like."

"Oh yes, I do," said Great Uncle Bulgaria, "why, when I was a young Womble we used to have *real* fogs which were so bad you couldn't see your front paw in front of your nose. Now just calm down while I tell you a little story.

"A long, long, LONG time ago when my fur was still grey I was out on the Common when a fog came rolling in. We used to call them pea-soupers in those days, because it was just like trying to find your way home through a bowl of thick pea soup. It was very, very frightening indeed and for a moment or two I thought I was going to be lost for ever. But *I'd* been taught, as you have, how to deal with dangers. So I looked round for the nearest thick tree and I climbed up it. Up and up I went until I reached the very top, and by that time I was so high I was clear of the fog. I could see it swirling and whirling down below me – because fog, as you know, always lies close to the ground – but I was in nice, clear air, so I soon stopped choking.

"Well, that was all right, I was safe. The only trouble was that in those days a London fog could sometimes last for a whole week, so after a while I began to worry that I might starve to death. It was a very nasty thought indeed. . ."

"Oh – *awful!*" agreed Orinoco.

"It was," said Great Uncle Bulgaria, his little eyes twinkling. "But then, all of a sudden, there was a *'whoosh'* and a *'swoosh'* of wings and the next moment I found myself looking at two bright yellow eyes. I was so surprised I nearly let go of the tree. I'd never seen this strange

creature before, but I tried to be polite and I said, 'Good evening'. The yellow eyes blinked and the creature opened its beak and replied. It said 'Wooooo. Wooooo.' It was a somewhat strange sound and it made my fur stand up on end. Then the creature jerked its head quite crossly and fluffed up its wings. I didn't understand what it meant at all until it got hold of my scarf with its beak and pulled.

"'Oh, you want me to follow you?' I asked.

"'Woo!' was the reply. 'Woo, Wooo, Woooooo!'

"And it pulled so hard and looked so stern that I forgot to be frightened and did exactly as it ordered. I climbed down the tree with my new friend flying round and round me and, as soon as my back

paws reached the ground, he grabbed hold of the end of my scarf and began to flutter forward. Now it was the most extraordinary thing that, although it was like running through a thick bowl of pea soup, it didn't seem to worry my friend at all. He swerved this way and that way, with me panting and choking along behind him, but never once did we run into a bush or hit a tree.

"On and on and on we went and quite a lot of the time I had my eyes tightly shut, because the yellow fog made them sting. But it didn't seem to bother my friend at all. I hadn't the faintest idea in which direction I was running, or where I was; and, although I was quite fit, I soon began to feel tired out and then, just

when I didn't think I could run another step, my friend let go of my scarf and *bang, crash, wallop,* I hit something solid. It was the front door of the burrow.

"'Woo, Wooo, Woooo,' said my friend, and for a second I saw his bright yellow eyes and heard the *swish-swish* of his wings and then he had vanished into the fog.

"'Thank you, thank you very much,' I said in a very breathless voice and I stumbled into the burrow where everybody was waiting for me. Oh I *was* glad to be home safe and sound. And much, much later, after a very good supper..."

"Ahhhh," said Orinoco, rubbing his fat little stomach.

"After a very good supper," went on Great Uncle Bulgaria, "when I'd told everybody about my adventure, I learnt that I'd been rescued by a very wise old owl who lived on the highest tree on Wimbledon Common. This owl was so old that he could not only see perfectly in the dark, he could also see in the thickest pea soup fog. And I think. . ."

"Hang on a minute, Bulgaria," said Tobermory, "there's somebody at the front door. It'll be young Bungo, I'll be bound."

And it was. Choking and panting and snuffling Bungo came thumping into the Workshop with his tidy-bag clasped in his paw.

"I say," wheezed Bungo, "it's ever so nice being home safe and sound. I'll tell you what, you'll never believe what's happened to me. This horrible yellow fog came right down on top of me, so I climbed up the nearest tree and I was

just starting to get worried about missing supper when. . ."

"Woosh, swoosh, and you found yourself looking at two bright yellow eyes . . ." said Wellington, Tomsk and Orinoco all together.

Bungo looked so surprised that everybody burst out laughing.

"S-sorry," said Wellington, "we're not laughing at *you*. It's just jolly nice to have you back, thanks to Mr. Owl, and what's more. . ."

"It's half-past suppertime," said Orinoco. "Come on! Race you to the kitchen!"

A Spelling Bee

T is for Tobermory,
So clever with his paws,
H is for the Hedgerows,
Where grow the hips and haws.

E is for Elderberries,
To make puddings and pies,
W is for Wellington,
Who never tells lies.

O is for Orinoco,
Oh, he's so lazy, too!
M is for Madame Cholet,
A cook well-known to you.

B is for Bulgaria,
With his warm tartan shawl,
L is for the autumn Leaves,
Which on the Common fall.

E is for Excitement,
Like when Tomsk was up a tree,
S is for Silver Womble,
The motor car made by Tobermory.

Put all the letters together,
And you will surely see,
People like Bungo and Shansi,
For they spell THE WOMBLES plain as can be!

FIND THE MYSTERY WOMBLE

Each of these objects represents a sport. Do you know what they are? If you do, fill in the names in the squares, and then read down the line of coloured squares to find the name of the mystery Womble. The pictures will give you a clue, but if you can't work it out for yourself turn to page 60 for the Answer.

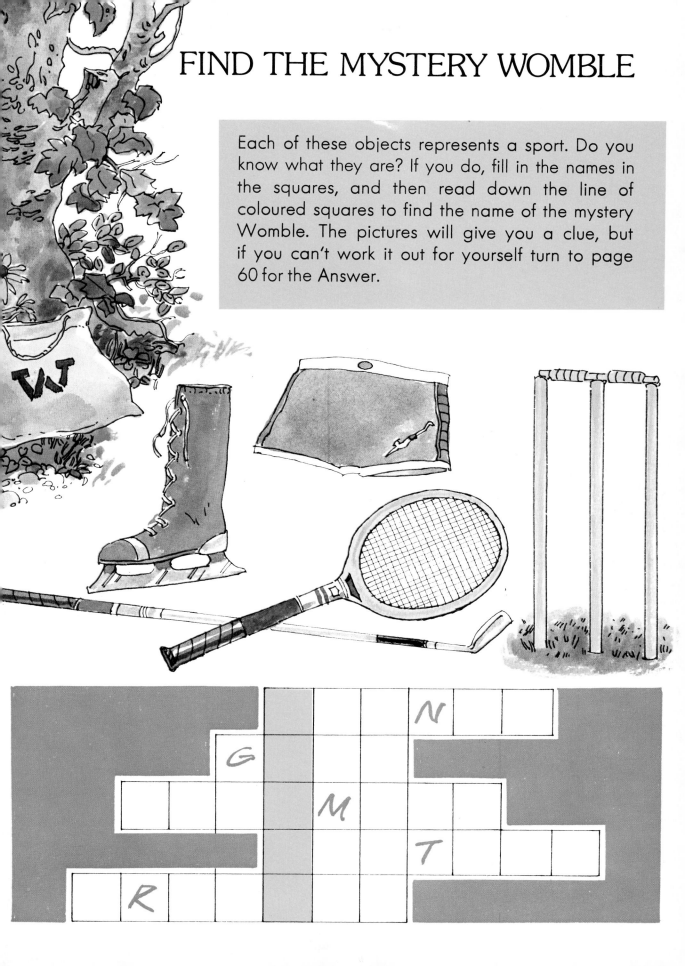

ANIMAL CRACKERS

Although the Wombles are on something less than friendly terms with some of their neighbours in the animal world, they still make a habit of learning about them and trying to understand them. Tobermory has even made models of some of the more exotic animals he has seen in books.

Try solving these animal puzzles and see if you know as much about animals as the Wombles do.

Which animal eats which food? Draw a line to match them up.

Name the animals that rhyme with these objects, then draw them.

Two of these animals have spots, and two have stripes. Why don't you draw them on?

Which animals are the mothers of the babies?

And now here's how Tobermory built a model lion. Why don't you have a go, it's very easy and all you need is an egg box, a toilet roll tube, some glue and some wool.

First cut out one of the cups on the egg box, and four strips from along the edge to use as legs. Paint every-thing yellow, and stick some yellow wool on one end of the toilet roll as shown. Stick the legs on, and another piece of wool for the tail. Paint a face on the cup, stick that on the roll and there you are – one fierce lion to play with!

Turn to page 60 to check your answers

I Spy...Tobermory's Workshop

The Wimbledon Burrow wouldn't be the comfortable home it is without Tobermory's wonderful Workshop. From its stores he is able to provide anything a Womble could possibly want, and his marvellous inventions make sure that the burrow is warm, well lit and safe.

Here is a picture of just some of the many items that the Wombles have collected over the years. How many of them begin with 'S'? You should be able to see at least twelve.

Check your answers on page 60

SHANSI'S SURPRISE

When Shansi returned from a litter-collecting expedition she had quite a haul in her litter bag. There was a cup, a pan, a glove, a bell, a tiny ornamental dragon, a sun from a charm bracelet and two little toy animals.

Imagine Shansi's surprise when Wellington pointed out that all the objects she had collected could be found in the names of flowers – flowers she could well have seen that day!

Do you know what the flowers were? Check your Answers on page 60.

15

Wellington and the Green Machine

by Elisabeth Beresford

Wellington had been very busy for some time in the Back Workshop. He had put a notice on the door which read: SORRY. KEEP OUT. INVENTING SOMETHING. So everybody did as they were asked, although they all wondered between themselves what he could possibly be doing.

"Perhaps it's something really important like an instant snack bar," said Orinoco hopefully.

"Or a clockwork golf set," suggested Tomsk, who was having trouble with his putting.

"I expect it's a super-cleaner-upper," said Bungo, "which will mean we'll never have to use tidy-bags ever again."

"What I'd like," said Tobermory, "is some light green paint. I need it for the outside of the burrow, which is getting very shabby. Very shabby indeed. Problems, problems. . ."

"As for me," sighed Madame Cholet, "I would like *le* washing machine. It is most tiring having to do all *le* washing, even though Alderney and Shansi help me. Eh, little ones?"

Alderney and Shansi nodded violently.

"Well, I daresay we'll soon know," said Great Uncle Bulgaria. "There hasn't been any hammering or banging noise for at least half-an-hour."

And, as usual, he was perfectly right, for that very same evening Wellington announced at suppertime that his new invention was finished and ready for inspection. It was a very strange object,

16

for it was made out of a petrol drum, an old fashioned mangle, part of a record player and several pieces of plastic tubing.

"Very impressive," said Great Uncle Bulgaria, "very impressive *indeed*. But – er – what is it, exactly?"

"A washing machine," said Wellington proudly. "The water comes in here, and goes out there. You set the record player dial here where it says Dirty Laundry, Very Dirty Laundry, Awful Laundry. Press that switch, pour in the daisy soap, press the second switch and the mangle goes round and round. It's quite simple really."

There was a stunned silence while everybody looked at the washing machine. Tobermory stroked his moustache and seemed about to say something, but he stopped himself.

"I'll give you a demonstration, if you like," said Wellington. "But first of all I must have something to wash."

Several Wombles shuffled their back paws and looked at each other and there was another pause until Great Uncle Bulgaria stepped forward and said:

"You shall have my MacWomble tartan shawl. It has got rather grubby recently. Here you are, Wellington."

"I say, thanks awfully," said Wellington. "Goodness, dear me, well, here goes. . . ."

Little Shansi slipped off and went and got Great Uncle Bulgaria's best shawl to put round his shoulders, as she knew that he felt the cold rather a lot. By the time she got back with it, everybody else was crouched at one end of the room watching the machine, which was hissing and bubbling and sending up clouds and clouds of bright green bubbles.

"What is the matter?" Shansi whispered to her best friend, Alderney.

"It won't stop," Alderney replied.

"Wellington knows how to make his invention begin washing clothes, but he forgot to put a stop button into it. It may go on and on washing Great Uncle Bulgaria's shawl for EVER!"

It was Tobermory, fighting his way through a cloud of bright green bubbles, who finally made the machine stop washing. He took a screw driver out of his apron pocket, turned this and that and with a last shudder the machine went quiet and the bubbles vanished. Very carefully Tobermory bent down and pulled out a strange, green-ish white piece of material.

"My MacWomble tartan shawl," exclaimed Great Uncle Bulgaria. *"Ho HUM."*

There was another very long silence this time.

"I can use it for dishcloths," said Madame Cholet. "It will be most useful, Monsieur Bulgaria. And you do 'ave two more new shawls in your cupboard, *tiens alors.*"

"I'm ever so sorry," said Wellington, in a small voice. "I was only trying to invent something useful."

"And so you have, young Womble," said Tobermory, dipping his front paw into the washing machine, "you've invented a nice, light green wash paint which is just what I need for redecorating the outside of the burrow. Ta very much!"

19

NAME THE TITLES

Wellington is one of the quietest, shyest Wombles in the burrow, and there is nothing he likes better than to get his nose into a good book. Here are just two of the books he has read lately. Can you guess the titles from the picture clues? Turn to page 60 for the Answers.

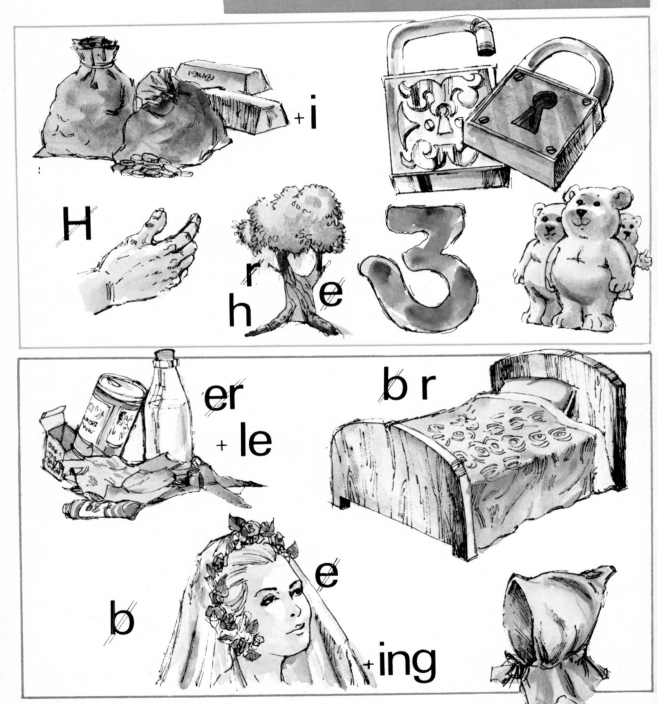

SPELL IT OUT

Great Uncle Bulgaria asked Tobermory to make him a sign. Tobermory got all the letters together and then . . . Oh no! He dropped them all on the ground!

Can you put all the same letters together, then spell out a famous Womble saying?

Turn to page 60 to check your answers

EVERY LETTER

Tomsk was just bringing back a full litter bag when – *rrrrrip!* – a hole appeared and everything fell out. Now just look at all the things in the Womble burrow!

Can you find something on this page for every letter of the alphabet? Turn to page 60 to see if you've missed anything.

PHOTO FIT

Wellington, Madame Cholet, Orinoco, Tobermory and Great Uncle Bulgaria all had their pictures taken. Unfortunately, when they had been developed, Tobermory left them on the kitchen table for Madame Cholet to look at.

That in itself wasn't unfortunate, but when Wellington dropped an old newspaper over them and then Orinoco rested on that newspaper to cut himself a great big slice of Dandelion pie, the result was tragic. All the photographs were cut in half.

Can you help the Wombles fit the correct halves together?

Check your answers on page 60

WELLINGTON WOMBLE'S 'W' PAGE

How many different objects can you find on this page? They all begin with 'W', and if you look closely you will see that there is an odd one out. Which is it? Look at page 60 to check your Answers.

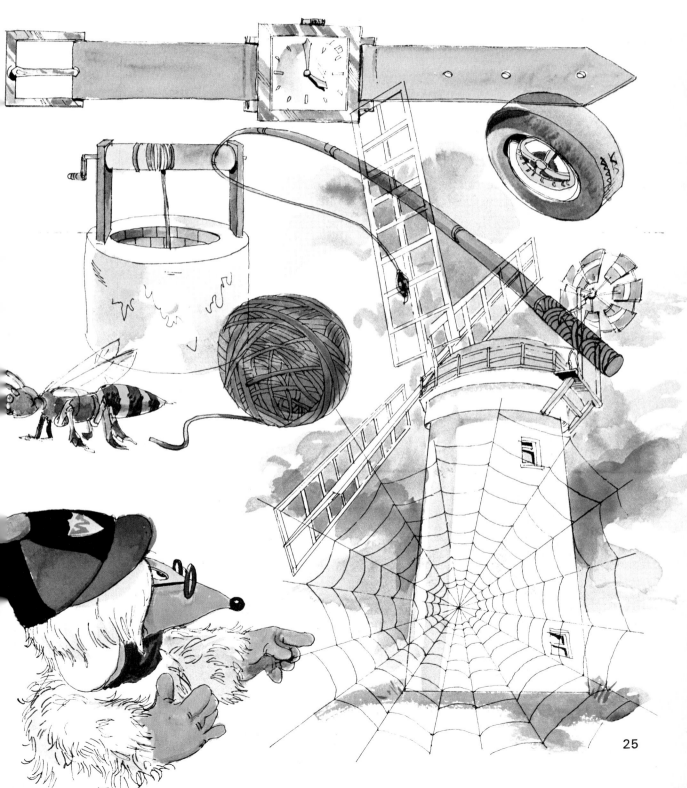

THE MACWOMBLE
HAS A SPOT OF TROUBLE

by Elisabeth Beresford

There had been a lot of cleaning and polishing going on in the Wimbledon Burrow, because The MacWomble was coming to stay.

"I don't know why we bother so much," grumbled Tobermory. "From what I remember of *his* burrow up at Loch Ness it's nothing very special. When I was there last I spent all my holiday repairing things. They hadn't got a door that fitted properly."

"Yes, yes, I daresay," agreed Great Uncle Bulgaria, "but I'm determined that my Wimbledon Wombles shall make a good impression. Now go away and tidy the Workshop while I finish my letters."

"Fuss, fuss, fuss," muttered Tobermory. But he went off just the same, because he wasn't going to have any Scottish Womble telling *him* how to run a Workshop.

Many of the other Wombles were feeling rather like Tobermory as they scurried about, sweeping and dusting and putting things straight.

As for Madame Cholet, she was practically going around in circles as she looked up special Scottish recipes and then tried them out one by one.

"Cold salad AGAIN?" said Orinoco at dinnertime.

"Since when has a salad been hot, hm?" demanded Madame Cholet. "Now sit down and eat up." She tapped Orinoco on the head with a wooden spoon as she hurried back to the stove to taste her latest Scottish dish.

"Goodness I'm tired," said little Alderney. "It's no fun at all working in the kitchen at the moment. Madame Cholet keeps saying 'do this, get that, mix the soup, stir the bracken'. My back paws are aching dreadfully!"

"I've had to polish all the tools in the Workshop," said Wellington gloomily.

"And I've had to polish the floor in the dormitory," put in Tomsk. "AND make my bed three times."

There was silence for a moment or two while everybody ate steadily, and then

Bungo, who had been very quiet for him, said loudly: "Well, I'm jolly glad The MacWomble's coming. *I* like The Mac-Womble."

"We all like The MacWomble," said Great Uncle Bulgaria overhearing these words. "And tomorrow, first thing, I want you all out on the Common to welcome him, with your fur neatly brushed. Bed early!"

The following morning they heard The MacWomble arriving long before he actually came into sight. It was quite misty on the Common, and everybody's fur tingled as they heard the distant skirl of bagpipes. They all stood to attention as this strange Scottish music grew nearer and nearer and then out of the mist strode the large, round figure of Cairngorm The MacWomble the Terrible, with the pipes over his shoulder and his MacWomble tartan swinging.

"Welcome," said Great Uncle Bulgaria, stepping forward.

The pipes moaned into silence and The MacWomble took off his bonnet and bowed.

"I'm glad to be here with my bonny wee Wimbledon Womble relations," roared The MacWomble. "You've not enlarged the burrow, I see. It's still rather a small, wee, poky place compared to mine. Lead on, Bulgaria."

The MacWomble strode down the

curious roundish-shaped white THING.

"It's a bracken haggis," said The Mac-Womble, "the best Womble food in the whole wor-r-rld. As soon as I've inspected yon burrow I'll show you how to cook it. You're all going to enjoy it very much."

"Thank you," said Madame Cholet faintly.

The MacWomble did indeed inspect the burrow and in spite of everybody's hard work he still found several things wrong with it.

Great Uncle Bulgaria, who is always polite, somehow managed to go on being polite, but Tobermory retired into his Workshop and put a notice on the door which said: BUSY. NO ENTRY. Everybody else hurried off to do something or other so that they could keep out of the way.

The last place that The MacWomble visited was the kitchen and here at least he found nothing wrong. He complimented Madame Cholet several times and then picked up the bracken haggis.

"Now, Madame Cholet," he boomed, "we'll cook this. I'll just show you how."

"Well, well, I'll be off. Work to do," said Great Uncle Bulgaria, and left hastily.

"Are you sure you know how to – er – cook le haggis?" asked Madame Cholet nervously.

"Aye. Nothing to it. Will you be so kind as to pass me yon big cook pan, please?"

One by one, as though drawn by a magnet, the young Wombles returned from the Common and gathered outside

lines of waiting Wombles, shaking each by his or her front paw until he came to Madame Cholet.

"It's glad I am to see you again," he boomed. "I've brought you a present all the way from Scotland."

"Oh, M'sieur MacWomble, how very kind," exclaimed Madame Cholet. "What is it? Oh dear! Oh me! *Tiens alors!*"

Madame Cholet stared, and so did everybody else, for The MacWomble had produced from his knapsack a the kitchen door. There seemed to be a lot of bumping and banging going on inside and the rumbling voice of The MacWomble was roaring away, with a *'tiens alors'* from Madame Cholet every now and then. She sounded more and more nervous.

Then there was a tremendous hissing noise . . . which was followed by a moment's silence, and then Madame Cholet's voice saying furiously: "Out, out, out of my kitchen. You have ruin-ed my best saucepan, also regard my nice clean floor which is clean no longer. Out, out, out!"

And something, which sounded remarkably like a saucepan being thrown very hard, went *'booooiiinnnggg'*.

The young Wombles took to their heels and ran for their lives.

Two seconds later, The MacWomble, who was splattered with some white, spongy-looking stuff, fairly burst out of the kitchen and raced down the corridor, with a wooden spoon whistling after him. He vanished in the direction of the Common.

Great Uncle Bulgaria and Tobermory very cautiously put their heads out into the corridor and listened to what Madame Cholet was saying to herself.

"Better leave her alone for a bit," Great Uncle Bulgaria said softly.

Two doors closed very, very gently.

Several hours passed. The Mac-Womble was playing a soft lament on his bagpipes on the far side of the Common when Bungo appeared.

"It's all right, wee Womble," said The MacWomble sadly. "I'll be away home soon. Nobody'll want me here any more after the mess my bracken haggis made of your nice kitchen. None of you'll speak to me again. Och well."

"'Course we're going to speak to you again," said Bungo. "Daresay an exploding haggis could happen to anyone. Anyway, Madame Cholet's cooled down now and we've cleaned out the kitchen good as new. Supper's ready and it's a special surprise . . . just for you. Come on."

It was a very special supper too. Absolutely delicious gorse and bracken porridge with moss salt for The Mac-Womble and buttercup syrup for everybody else.

"I'll tell you what," said The Mac-Womble, after he'd apologised at least three times about the haggis, "this, Madame Cholet, is the very best porridge I've ever tasted. You *are* the best Womble cook in the whole wor-r-rld."

"*Tiens alors,* it is nothing. Do 'ave a second helping," said Madame Cholet, "and welcome yet again to our 'umble Wimbledon Burrow."

"Hear, hear," said Great Uncle Bulgaria, "and here's to a happy holiday, MacWomble."

And it was.

A PUZZLING PAGE!

1.

Madame Cholet has baked one of her delicious herb and fir cone pies, and she wants to know how she can cut it into the biggest number of pieces – not all equal – with only four straight cuts. Can you help her?

2.

Miss Adelaide has woven this rug from scraps of wool, and round the edge she has embroidered the Womble motto, although as you can see, there is more to it than that! Beginning at the second W, read every other letter round the rug and go round twice to find the motto.

Check your answers on page 60

Wombles in Words and Pictures

1.
De-tail an animal,
Add something sweet,
Behead this twice,
Two vowels now this Womble complete.

2.
A very plain cake,
Plus a word rhyming with doe,
Names a mischievous young Womble,
That you're sure to know.

3.
This one's very easy,
It's the study of plants and flowers,
And also the name of an old Womble,
Who in the garden passes many hours.

4.
Take half of a fruit,
And add two thirds of the sky,
For the name of a Womble
Who says, "Good at golf am I!"

Check your answers on page 60

The Wombles are very particular eaters. They are strict vegetarians and they like to make use of the natural resources around them. That's why they like fruit, and plenty of it. Here are three questions about fruit.

FRUIT SALAD

1. Fill in the squares with the names of the fruit shown. If your answers are right, you will find the name of another fruit in the black box.

2. Which Womble's name is spelt here?

3. Which fruits rhyme with these objects?

Turn to page 60 to check your answers

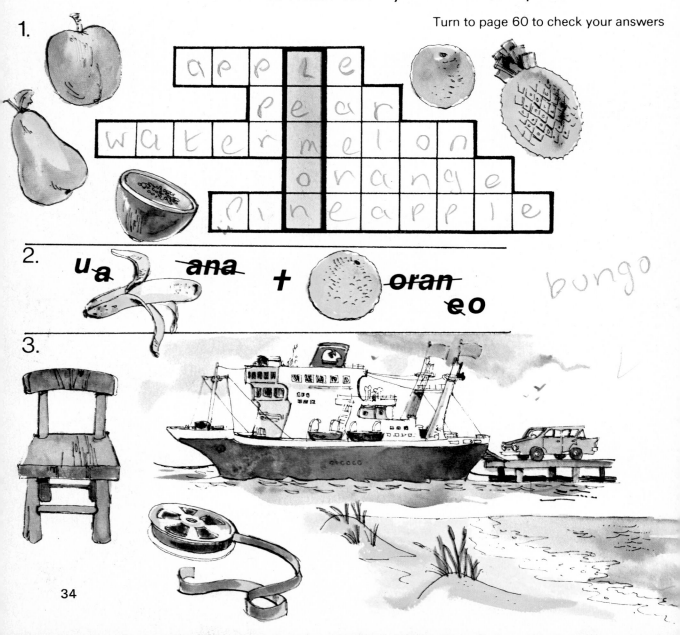

1.

a	p	p	l	e			
			p	e	a	r	
w	a	t	e	r	m	e	l	o	n
				o	r	a	n	g	e
	p	i	n	e	a	p	p	l	e

2.   u a   ~~ana~~   +   ~~oran~~
                              e o

bungo

3.

WHICH WOMBLE?

Here is Orinoco helping Madame Cholet in the kitchen. He doesn't look too happy, because he has been kept so busy that he hasn't had time to nibble any tit-bits, but Madame Cholet has a secret plate of chocolate pudding waiting for him when he has finished.

Take a good look at the numbered objects in the kitchen, then take the initial letter of each to spell the name of another Womble.

Check your answers on page 60

FOLLOW THE STARS

"What are you doing, Wellington?" asked Great Uncle Bulgaria, one windy, rainy evening.

Wellington didn't answer at first. He was just too busy! But at last he looked up from his work and replied: "I'm making a star-chart for my bedroom. You see, I get a bit confused when I look up at the sky and see all the stars, like hundreds and thousands on a Christmas cake; so I'm going to start learning about the constellations, and my chart will help me."

"What a very good idea! Then you'll be able to find the group of stars called The Plough . . . and even the Great Bear and the Little Bear!" Great Uncle Bulgaria remarked.

"I've never seen bears in the sky!" said Orinoco, sleepily, "but I suppose there are some if you say so."

While Great Uncle Bulgaria told Orinoco as much as he could about the stars, Wellington frowned hard and got on with his work. And this is what he did!

He found a large piece of cardboard and cut it into a big oblong. Then he got some dark blue cartridge paper and stuck it on top. After this he had to make lots of tiny silver stars out of silver paper – you could cheat by buying them in packets – which he glued on to his chart carefully, making different constellations.

Wellington's chart looked lovely and was very much admired. What about making one yourself, for your bedroom?

LITTLE BEAR

GREAT BEAR

TOMSK GETS A LETTER

Tomsk had just received a letter from Idaho Womble who lives in America in the enormous burrow which is run by Cousin Yellowstone Womble. Now it always takes Tomsk rather a long time to read anything, but he seemed to be having even more trouble than usual. First he held the letter at arm's length, and then he put it right up to the end of his nose. Next he turned it upside down and finally he put it on the ground and heaved a very big sigh.

Wellington, who had been watching this odd behaviour for the last ten minutes was, by now, almost bursting with curiosity.

by Elisabeth Beresford

"I say, Tomsk, old Womble," he said, "excuse me, but is Idaho's writing very difficult to understand?"

"Yes. It's not really writing-writing you see," replied Tomsk, "in fact it's not like any writing I've ever seen. Want to have a look?"

"Rather!" said Wellington, "I bet it's only . . . oh!"

Wellington's eyes grew as round as his spectacles as he stared at Idaho's letter. There weren't any words at all in it, only a lot of small pictures, and for the next few minutes Wellington behaved in exactly the same strange way as Tomsk had done. But he was no wiser at the end of it.

"What do you think you're doing?" asked Great Uncle Bulgaria, who had just come out onto the Common to enjoy the evening sunshine.

Tomsk and Wellington both tried to explain at once and Great Uncle Bulgaria looked over his spectacles at them until they had finished and then he went, "Ho hum, hum ho," and held out his white paw as he said: "What a lot of fuss about nothing. Allow me, young Wombles. I daresay it's quite a simple letter to understand and . . . oh!"

Great Uncle Bulgaria held the letter upside down and sideways on and right up to his spectacles, shaking his head.

"It's not real writing-writing, is it?" asked Tomsk.

"No, indeed," agreed Great Uncle Bulgaria. "Ah, Madame Cholet, good evening. I wonder if we could ask a favour of you?"

"*Tiens alors,* of course!" said Madame Cholet, who had popped out of the kitchen for a moment to cool down as she had got rather warm while cooking.

"As you are so good at reading foreign recipes, perhaps you will be able to translate this letter from our American Cousin Idaho," said Great Uncle Bulgaria.

"With pleasure," said Madame Cholet, "it is doubtless quite simple. But this is not *le* writing-writing! It is all pictures. No, this I cannot translate. Perhaps M'sieur Tobermory will be able to do so. He is

very clever at reading pink-prints."

"Blue-prints, I think you mean," said Great Uncle Bulgaria. "What a good idea, let us go and ask him at once!"

But Tobermory was just as puzzled by the letter as everyone else. He pinned it up on his notice-board and he stared at it from close to and then from far away, but it didn't do any good.

"Problems, problems," muttered Tobermory, "as if I haven't got enough to do without having to try and read this rigmarole. Why can't Idaho learn to write writing-writing like every other sensible Womble? It's probably some daft idea of Cousin Yellowstone's!"

Tobermory has always been rather jealous of Cousin Yellowstone for some reason.

"Ahem, excuse me," said a soft voice, and there was Miss Adelaide, who is in charge of the Womblegarten, standing in the doorway. Everybody else stopped talking at once, which is the effect Miss Adelaide always has on other Wombles, even Great Uncle Bulgaria.

"I understand," said Miss Adelaide, "that you are having a little difficulty reading a letter from one of our American relations. Perhaps you would allow me to have a look?"

Everybody stood respectfully to one side and Miss Adelaide went up to the notice-board and studied the letter.

"A picture of a heart, followed by a rather badly drawn paw and then what I take to be a telegram . . . dear me. Tck-tck-tck."

"Do you understand it, Miss Adelaide?" asked Great Uncle Bulgaria.

"Not exactly. But I believe I know somebody who will. Tomsk, run along to the Womblegarten, Class 2. At the very back of the class you will find a small Womble doing extra homework. I regret to say that he finds reading, writing and arithmetic very difficult. He spends all his spare time, and much of his school time too, pretending to be a Red Indian Womble."

In a very short time Tomsk returned, bringing with him a small tubby Womble who was clutching an exercise book in one paw and a rather gnawed pencil in the other. He looked very scared.

"Now then, little Womble," said Miss Adelaide, "instead of doing extra homework you can just read this letter for us. One, two, three, off you go."

The little Womble was so pleased to

hear that he wasn't in trouble he forgot to be nervous.

He went up to the notice-board, blinked his little round eyes and then said in a squeaky voice: "Heart – like, fondest, paw . . um . . telegram thing . . . oh yes, I see. The letter says 'Fondest paw greetings to all our Womble cousins in Britain from Idaho Red Indian Womble.' Please may I be excused now, Miss Adelaide?"

"Yes, indeed," said Miss Adelaide, "but wait for one moment. You did that very well."

The little Womble grinned from ear to ear and shuffled his back paws while everybody else stared at him in admiration.

"Tck-tck-tck," said Great Uncle Bulgaria, starting to laugh. "Here we are all the rest of us trying to be so clever, and it's taken this very small Womble to put us right! Thank you, small Womble. And I think I understand why Miss Adelaide wants you to wait. Will you help Tomsk to send a Red Indian Womble picture-writing message back to our relations in America?"

"Rather," said Tomsk and little Womble together and Tomsk added, "I think picture-writing is much more fun than writing-writing any day."

"*Tiens alors!*" said Madame Cholet with a chuckle. "In which case I too will give you a messsage. 'Three saucepans, two pie dishes, knives, forks, spoons and plates.' What does that mean?"

Everybody answered at once: "Suppertime!"

And it was.

WHOSE HATS?

There is quite an assortment of hats here, isn't there? Each one belongs to a Womble, but do you know which Womble? See how many you can identify.

a

e

b

d

c

Check your answers on page 60

Name the missing Womble

Here you see several well-known Wombles. If you take one letter from each of their names and rearrange them, you will find the name of another famous Womble.

Turn to page 60 to check your answer

A BUNDLE OF BUNS

Everyone has heard of the hot cross buns which we eat at Easter, but do you know:

1. The bun that is a Womble?

2. The bun that is a type of dwelling?

3. The bun that is a bird?

4. The bun that is a cork?

5. The bun that is a bed?

6. The bun that is a pet name for a rabbit?

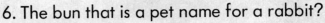

Check your answers on page 60.

Watch it!

Time is as important to the Wombles as it is to everybody else – that's why they have to check in and out of the burrow when they're collecting rubbish. But just because it's important to them doesn't mean that they can't have a joke about it, as Wellington discovered when he found a joke book.

Here are some of the jokes that were enjoyed in the Wombles' burrow.

When is a clock upstairs dangerous?
When it runs down and strikes one.

Who was the smallest man in history?
The sailor who went to sleep on his watch.

If you smashed a clock, could you be accused of killing time?
Not if the clock struck first.

Which insect never hears the alarm?
The deaf watch beetle.

How do you make time fly?
Throw a clock out of the window.

How does a witch tell the time?
With a witch watch.

Why should you always wear a watch in the desert?
Because it has a spring inside.

What's the difference between a jeweller and a jailer?
One sells watches and the other watches cells.

Capable Carrots

Madame Cholet doesn't have much time for anything but cooking, but just once in a while she takes time off to make things look prettier. Here's how she made hanging flowers out of the ends of two old carrots.

First Madame Cholet scooped out the middle of the carrot ends with a spoon. Then she bent a paper clip to fit in them as shown. She tied the clip to some cotton hanging from the ceiling and poured water into the carrot. Soon there were lovely green shoots dangling round her head. Why don't you try it – so long as you keep filling them up with water they will grow.

Another way of using carrots to give you some fun is by making them into desert islands. Wellington is particularly fond of doing this as he has always had an interest in pirates since he found a book called *Treasure Island*. You take some carrot ends and place them on a plate that has been filled with water. They soon look like islands with trees on them, and Wellington likes to push his tiny homemade boats around them, playing at pirates looking for buried treasure. Why don't you have a go?

ORINOCO AND THE HOOLA HOOP

by Elisabeth Beresford

Now if there is one thing that Tomsk is really good at, it's all kinds of games. He can play football, cricket, golf, tennis, rounders, hockey, ice-hockey and marbles better than any other Womble. He is also better at running, skating, swimming, skiing and jumping.

"Come on, Orinoco," Tomsk rumbled one nice bright frosty morning when all the young Wombles had finished tidying-up work, "let's go and play some football."

"No, thanks. Jolly nice of you and all that," replied Orinoco, "but I've got a lot to do. I've got to catch up on my sleep for one thing. I only got about ten hours last night."

"Ten hours sleep is enough for any Womble," said Tomsk. "If you eat and sleep any more you'll get so fat you'll look like a round, furry football yourself."

"I'm a very good shape and size for a Womble," replied Orinoco, and he walked off with his nose in the air. Unfortunately he didn't look where he was going and the next moment he found himself sliding down a steep bank.

"Help, *whoops, ouch,*" shouted Orinoco, rolling over and over until, with a final, *"OOOOO-EH!"*, he splashed straight into Queen's Mere, sending showers of muddy water in all directions.

"Ho, ho, ho," rumbled Tomsk, roaring with laughter and holding his sides. "Are you all right, Orinoco?"

"'Course I'm all right," replied Orinoco crossly, because like all the Wombles he can swim well. And he paddled off towards the bank with his front paws simply churning up the water; but the strange thing was that, although he was now swimming as fast as he could, he seemed to be staying in the same place.

"I can't . . ." puffed Orinoco, "get any further. Help . . . I'm trapped. A monster's got hold of me. *Puff, puff, puff.* It's going to drag me down. Heeeelp."

Tomsk stopped laughing and ran down the bank and did a perfect dive which left hardly a ripple on the water. Down and down he went until he got to the bottom of the pond where Orinoco's little back paws were trapped by something which felt rather like a very strong eel. Tomsk pulled and tugged and there was a sucking, squelching noise and the next moment Orinoco was free and swimming like a champion and he didn't stop until he was back on nice, safe, dry land.

"*Ho, ho, ho,*" rumbled Tomsk, swimming after him, "you're all right, Orinoco. Here's your monster. It's just an old plastic hoop. Look!"

"Tomsk does everything better than I do," said Orinoco, "except perhaps eating and sleeping. I just wish there was one game that I could be good at, only a Womble of my shape just can't play football or golf or even marbles very well."

"Ho hum," said Tobermory, hiding a smile. "Well, perhaps a little bit of exercise might be a good thing for you, Orinoco. You don't want to get too fat, after all. And with your shape maybe using that hoop would be a good idea. Now then, put it over your head, hold it in your front paws, swing the hoop round

Orinoco took off his hat and wrung it out and then he shook himself so that little drops of water flew in all directions. He felt crosser than ever and very silly, too, because now he'd made a fool of himself twice over in front of Tomsk. Once by falling down the bank and secondly he'd been caught by a monster; only it wasn't a monster at all, just a stupid old hoop.

"Thank you for rescuing me," said Orinoco coldly, and he trotted off towards the burrow with Tomsk pounding along behind him bowling the hoop. Orinoco was very quiet for the rest of the day and early next morning he went to see Tobermory to tell him all his troubles.

and see if you can make it bounce in a circle off your tummy. One, two, three, go. . ."

Orinoco tried it and the first few times the hoop just fell to the ground. And then he got a little better at it, and then better still and in a few minutes he found he could make the hoop spin round and round his tubby little body. It was quite hard work, but it was great fun at the same time.

"Well done, young Womble. You've really got just the right figure for hoola-hooping," said Tobermory. "Off you go and challenge Tomsk."

And do you know, the funny thing is that, although Tomsk is really good at all kinds of games, he never can spin the hoola hoop as well as Orinoco does. In fact Orinoco is the champion hoola hoop spinner of the burrow.

The only problem is that taking all that exercise seems to make him even more hungry and even sleepier than ever!

TOBERMORY'S GIFT

...s a small chest for a doll's house
... or, if you prefer, an ear-ring chest.

...bermory made one for Madame Cholet for
...ristmas – and she loved it.

...u'll need . . .

...hree large empty matchboxes
...bright sticky paper
...hree paper fasteners (brass) for knobs

...ake out the matchbox drawers and decorate the front,
...back and sides with your sticky paper.

...Now decorate the top of your No. 1 matchbox, and the
...bottom of your No. 3 matchbox.

...lace a brass paper fastener at the front of each of the three
...drawers. Now glue your three matchboxes together.

...ut your drawers back, and there you are – finished.

51

MAKE IT AND SEE

What do the Wombles do with all their litter? It's a question that's often been asked. We all know about the new rockers on Great Uncle Bulgaria's chair which were made from old tyres, and the damp newspapers they use for growing mushrooms, but surely they can't make use of every single little bit of rubbish they find? What would they do, for instance, with a crate full of empty bottles, a set of handlebars, a pile of yoghurt cartons?

Here's exactly what those ingenious creatures did with these objects. Why don't you try doing something similar?

MADAME CHOLET'S IDEA

Well, the bottles were easy. Madame Cholet washed them all out very carefully, rinsed them, washed them again and left them to dry. Then she filled them up with her delicious dandelion cordial, so that every time the Wombles wanted to have a drink she could just pour one straight from the bottle instead of doing all that boiling and extracting and adding sugar, just for one tiny cupful.

TOBERMORY'S MONSTER

The handlebars were more difficult, and it's true that for nearly a week they weren't used for anything other than propping up a shelf of books in the Womble library. And then, one night after supper, while the Wombles were talking just before going to bed, there was a tremendous shuddering that shook the entire burrow. Tomsk popped his head outside to see what it was, and there, standing over him and snorting in the light of the moon was a great big bull.

Now bulls have nothing particular against the Wombles, but they're such clumsy creatures and they hardly ever look where they are putting their feet. When there's a bull wandering around, nothing is safe. It could quite easily squash the burrow just by running over it. Tomsk went back in and told the others, and after a long conversation and a rather good idea from Tobermory, they had soon solved the problem of the bull and what to do with the handlebars.

First, Tobermory put an old broom handle into the handlebars, and then Wellington, who has very steady

paws, drew a picture of the most terrifying bull you have ever seen on a large piece of plastic sheeting. He wrapped this round a football and stuck it onto the handlebars.

After that Tobermory tied string round the ends of the handlebars and pulled it round some trees near the Womble burrow. Then he laid the broom handle, football, handlebars and plastic sheeting on the ground. The next day, when the bull blundered towards the Womble burrow, he barged into the string. *Whoosh!* Quick as a flash the string pulled the handlebars up, and there, facing the bull, was the most fearsome creature he'd seen. He made sure he didn't stray there too often, and whenever he did there was Tobermory's monster to frighten him.

TO HELP TOMSK

The yoghurt cartons were next. There were so many of them that

Tobermory once worked a full week trying to build things with them. He sound-proofed his Workshop with them, he gave Madame Cholet a big pile for her jam, and he even planted nine of them in the grass outside the burrow so that Tomsk could practise his putting.

But there were still plenty left, and it was only when Tomsk came to him with a request, that Tobermory found yet another way of using them. Tomsk you see, had taken up wrestling.

As you will know, wrestling is not

limbs, and at the joints he just tied a piece of string through. In the end the dummy looked something like this:

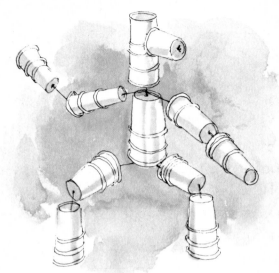

Although after Tomsk had been practising for a while it looked more like this:

the gentlest of sports and Tomsk found it difficult to persuade any of the other Wombles to let him practise his holds on them. He had to practise, but he had no one to practise on. What he needed was a dummy with moveable parts.

And that's exactly what Tobermory built for him. He stuck lots of the cartons inside each other to make the

Well, that's what the Wombles did with three different kinds of litter. Why don't you see what you can make out of things that would otherwise be thrown away? Just think what the shape of them suggests to you, then go right ahead. Good luck!

PERFECT PICTURES

Have you ever wanted to paint a really detailed picture in miniature?

Here's what Tobermory made for Orinoco.

First of all he found a big empty coffee tin. He took the lid off and made a small hole right in the middle of the bottom. Next thing he did was to tie some greaseproof paper over the open end.

Last of all, he fixed it on top of a table and pointed the end with the hole in it out of the window, where a tree stood in the sun.

Orinoco complained at first because the picture on the greaseproof paper was upside down, but after he had painted it and turned it round he changed his mind. The picture was nearly perfect!

ALDERNEY'S APPLE CANDLE HOLDER

One day Bungo and the other young Wombles decided to hold a Hallowe'en Party. Madame Cholet had plenty of apples for the ducking game, and Alderney used several of the apples to make candle holders so that they could play games by candlelight.

Apple candle holders are simple and easy to make and are great fun for a Hallowe'en party.

You need one large firm red apple, polished hard so that it shines, a small candle and a saucer.

Ask Mummy to cut a deep hole in the apple, just small enough to hold the candle. Make sure that the cut is at the stem end of the apple. Place the candle in a saucer, and if you are going to light it later add a little water.

READ ALL ABOUT IT

It was a very, very windy day when it happened. Although the sun was shining, the wind was like a fury, whipping off hats, waggling scarves, whisking wads of paper high into the air. It was on one of these pieces of paper that Wellington found a list. From what he could gather it was a list of books.

When he got back to the burrow he found that Tomsk had also found a list – or rather the list had found Tomsk by blowing straight into his litter bag – and Tomsk's list appeared to be a list of authors. That night the Wombles tried to match the titles of the books with the authors. Why don't you try?

Robbery!
Know your vegetables
Learn to spell
Underwater plants
Tragedy on the cliffs
The star spangled banner
All about animals
Mystery theft
The library books
Tied up
Summer treat
Practical jokes
The hard seat

I. Scream
Maida Stone
Red M. Hall
P. Zargreen
Major Laff
Anne Dover D'moni
Alf A. Bett
Noah Zark
C. Weed
Eileen Dover
Grannie Knott
Tarzan Tripes
Hugh Dunnit

Great Uncle Bulgaria and the GREAT STORM

by Elisabeth Beresford

It was a very wild and stormy night with a strong wind blowing across Wimbledon Common and all the Wombles were very glad that they were safe and snug inside the burrow.

"Dear me," said Great Uncle Bulgaria, helping himself to some more salted acorns, "it reminds me of the great storm, many years ago, when I was quite a young Womble. But I don't suppose you'll want to hear about that."

At which all the young Wombles in the Playroom stopped eating their salted acorns and nodded their heads. It was just the right sort of night for listening to one of the old Womble's stories.

"Very well then," said Great Uncle Bulgaria, "once upon a time, a long, long time ago, a great wind blew up. It was so strong that it blew the roofs off houses and it made every tree on the Common bend over sideways. It blew a lot of us young Wombles off our back paws, too, and it sent us flying across the grass like so many little furry balls of fluff. Head over back paws we went in all directions, but luckily we all got back to the burrow safe and sound. We shut the front door and had a nice supper and told a few stories and we were just about ready to go to bed when we heard a dreadful roaring, groaning noise and we knew that one of the biggest trees on the Common was going to be blown over.

"All we young Wombles were very, very frightened indeed, because the burrow wasn't as soundly built then as it is now, and we knew that if the tree fell on top of our roof it might bring the ceilings crashing down. It might even destroy some of the burrow completely."

"OOOOh," went everybody as Great Uncle Bulgaria paused to have a sip of hot elmbark juice. And Wellington looked anxiously at the strong wooden beams that criss-crossed the Playroom ceiling. They looked secure enough, but you never knew!

"Anyway," went on Great Uncle Bulgaria, "before we had time to get really scared out of our fur we were given our marching orders. We were all roped together, like so many mountain-climbers, and Great Aunt Thessaly, who was in charge of us, led the way out onto the Common. The wind was roaring and the great tree was lashing about as though it was only a blade of grass. Backwards and forwards it went, creaking and groaning so loudly it even drowned the noise of the storm. Its enormous roots were being dragged out of the ground and it was a truly awful sight. But Great Aunt Thessaly was as cool as a buttercup shake. She watched and waited and then, just as there was a gust of wind of gigantic force, she raised her arm and pointed and we all rushed forward together and threw ourselves at the tree as it was leaning away from us and the burrow. We clambered up its great trunk, hanging on with our front and back paws as tightly as we could, and just for a moment the tree started to swing back again, but with our added weight the wind couldn't lift it. I, for one, closed my eyes and I'm sure everybody else did too and then there was a final groaning sound and the tree fell forwards and lay still with all its branches rustling round it. It was a sad moment, as it always is when a tree falls, but we all knew that it would have

ANSWERS

FIND THE MYSTERY WOMBLE

Tennis, Golf, Swimming, Skating, Cricket. The mystery Womble is Tomsk.

ANIMAL CRACKERS

Which food? 1 – B, 2 – A, 3 – D, 4 – E, 5 – C. Rhymes: Boat – goat, wig – pig, hat – bat, cat, chair – bear, pen – hen, log – dog, house – mouse. Who's mother? 1 – B, 2 – C, 3 – F, 4 – G, 5 – H, 6 – E, 7 – D, 8 – A.

I SPY . . . TOBERMORY'S WORKSHOP

Shelves, suitcase, socks, shoes, sticks, scarves, sweater, skate, satchel, screwdriver, saw, sunglasses, a shirt and a spade.

SHANSI'S SURPRISE

Dandelion, pansy, buttercup, foxglove, cowslip, snapdragon, bluebell, sunflower.

NAME THE TITLES

Goldilocks and the Three Bears; Little Red Riding Hood.

SPELL IT OUT

Remember you're a Womble.

EVERY LETTER

Among other things, the picture includes an apple, book, chair, door, egg, face, Great Uncle Bulgaria, hole, ice cream, jam, kettle, litter bag, mousetrap, newspaper, Orinoco, pipe, queen, rope, shoe, Tomsk, umbrella, violin, Wellington, xylophone, yacht, zebra.

PHOTO FIT

A & 4, B & 1, C & 5, D & 3, E & 2.

WELLINGTON WOMBLE'S 'W' PAGE

Watch; wheel; windmill; well; whip; wasp; web; wool. The wasp is the odd one out because it is the only living thing on the page.

A PUZZLING PAGE

1. 11 pieces.
2. The Womble motto is: Waste Not Want Not!

WOMBLES IN WORDS AND PICTURES

1. Bulgaria 2. Bungo 3. Botany 4. Tomsk.

FRUIT SALAD

1. Lemon. (Apple, pear, watermelon, orange, pineapple). 2. Bungo. 3. Pear (chair), grape (tape), cherry (ferry), peach (beach).

WHICH WOMBLE?

3. Tray, 5. Onion, 1. Marrow, 4. Spoon, 2. Kettle, TOMSK.

WHOSE HATS

a) Great Uncle Bulgaria; b) Bungo; c) Tobermory; d) Madame Cholet; e) Orinoco.

NAME THE MISSING WOMBLE

Y from Tobermory, E from Madame Cholet, L from Great Uncle Bulgaria, L from MacWomble, O from Orinoco, W from Wellington, S from Tomsk, T from Botany, O from Bungo, N from Alderney, E from Miss Adelaide-YELLOWSTONE.

A BUNDLE OF BUNS

1. Bungo. 2. Bungalow. 3. Bunting. 4. Bung. 5. Bunk. 6. Bunny.

fallen anyway and we *had* stopped it crushing our burrow.

"We were all very glad to get back home and, what with the scare and the excitement of it all, we slept the clock round. But the following night – which was clear and calm without a trace of wind – Great Aunt Thessaly had us out on the Common again, working as hard as we could on the tree. In those days, of course, Wombles knew how to work. *Ho hum.*"

Great Uncle Bulgaria had another sip of elmbark and his old eyes twinkled as the Wombles in the Playroom all nudged each other and chuckled behind their paws at these familiar words.

"Hello, hello," said Tobermory putting his head round the door, "what are you lot all giggling about? Any salted acorns left for me then? Well, the storm has died down a bit, or have you all been so busy chattering that you hadn't noticed, eh?"

Five minutes later all the young Wombles but one had gone happily trotting off to bed. The one who was left was Wellington.

"Excuse me, Great Uncle Bulgaria," he said." Sorry to ask, but what did you have to do to the tree?"

"Use your eyes, young Womble," said Great Uncle Bulgaria, "and look up at the ceiling. See those good, strong beams up there? Well, that's part of the great tree which fell over in the storm. The rest of it is all round you in the doors and the walls and that's why our burrow is so safe, snug and secure today. We put that tree to very good use, instead of burning it out on the Common as those wasteful Human Beings would have done. But then in my young days. . ."

"I know," said Wellington, quite cheekily for him, "in your young days Wombles knew how to work. *Ho hum.* Goodnight, Great Uncle Bulgaria, and thank you for telling us a jolly nice story."

61

THE VANISHING CAP

A game for 2 or more players.

It's been a long working day, and now all the Wombles are back in the burrow, preparing for tea. Everyone is happy until – oh no! – Bungo has lost his cap!

But where? Bungo isn't quite sure. It might have been by that broken tree where he found the yoghurt cartons, or maybe it was at the pond where he found that large plastic bag. It might have been at the hill, or near that abandoned car, or under the oak tree where he stopped for a short rest. Bungo just can't quite remember.

BROKEN TREE

START HERE

YOGHURT CARTON